S0-ARJ-990

For my darling son Matthew –
I love you right up to the stars and back.

An Imprint of Sterling Publishing
387 Park Avenue South
New York, NY 10016

SANDY CREEK and the distinctive Sandy Creek logo
are registered trademarks of Barnes & Noble, Inc.

Text and illustrations © 2005 by Trace Moroney

This 2012 custom edition is published exclusively for Sandy Creek by The Five Mile Press.

All rights reserved. No part of this publication may be reproduced, stored in a retrieval system, or
transmitted, in any form or by any means, electronic, mechanical, photocopying, recording, or otherwise,
without prior written permission from the publisher.

ISBN: 978 1 4351 4520 7

Manufactured in Heshan City, Guangdong Province, China

Lot #:
2 4 6 8 10 9 7 5 3 1
10/12

The Big Book of
Love

Written and illustrated by Trace Moroney

Sandy Creek
NEW YORK

Love feels like hundreds of butterflies
dancing in my heart.

Love makes me want to dance and sing and climb the highest mountain, and shout ...

I love

Love is a warm, **fuzzy**,
safe feeling.

Love is *the* most special gift
you can give someone else.

When I love someone I want
to take care of them,
and make sure I don't do
anything to hurt them.

When someone loves me
it helps make my worries
go away!

I especially love my Mom and Dad,

my dog Poppy . . .

and my best friend, Scarlet.

I also love . . .
ice cream,

spaghetti,

and strawberries.

And . . . there are lots of things
I love about being me!

LOVING YOUR CHILD

The love that a parent feels for his or her child is like no other, and is profoundly deep. There is a biological reason for the strength of this love – to encourage us as parents to provide our children with guidance, support and *protection* and to help shape them into healthy, happy and *independent* adults.

The greatest gift you can give your child is healthy self-esteem. Children who feel valued, accepted and have a sense of belonging feel good about themselves.

Being demonstrative in our love for our children provides the core foundation, or building-blocks, in developing their self-esteem.

This can be done in many ways – by spending one-on-one time, listening to issues or problems, praising good behavior or a task well done and offering support and guidance in a productive and non-threatening way.

There are many non-verbal ways of demonstrating love, including hugs, kisses and smiles.

And the most precious and empowering words your child can hear from you are 'I love you'.

TRACE MORONEY